I once found a leaf that looked like a star.
"I'm going to bring this for show-and-tell," I told
my mother.
"Don't you think it's kind of small?" she asked.

SHOW-AND-TELL

BARNEY SALTZBERG

HYPERION BOOKS FOR CHILDREN
NEW YORK

This book is for my mother and father, Ruth and Irv,
who once gave me an Italian metallic orange-and-green
folding bicycle and who have always encouraged me
to follow my dreams!

A special thanks to Phoebe Souza,
who has such style.
And, as always, Joy, George, and
Peggy Rathmann, my Angels.

Printed in Hong Kong.
For information address Hyperion Books for Children,
114 Fifth Avenue, New York, New York 10011.
First Edition
1 3 5 7 9 10 8 6 4 2

Saltzberg, Barney.
Show-and-tell/Barney Saltzberg — 1st ed.
p. cm.
Summary: Phoebe discovers a way to avoid her parents'
meddling in show-and-tell time at school.
ISBN 0-7868-0020-8 (trade) — ISBN 0-7868-2016-0 (lib. bdg.)
[1. Schools — Fiction. 2. Parent and child — Fiction.] I. Title.
PZ7.S1552Sh 1994
[E] — dc20   93-47365   CIP   AP

The artwork for each picture is prepared using
mixed media on Seth Cole paper.
This book is set in 17-point American Typewriter.

My parents went out and bought me a palm tree from Northern Ooboonie. I knew I'd be embarrassed bring-ing something so big to school, but they spent all that money. What else could I do?

During show-and-tell,
Rebecca shared one
of her inventions. She
said it would keep paper
from blowing away.
It was a rock.

Josh shared his trumpet
and played a song he wrote
about his dog.

Everyone in the class
shared something. Finally
Ms. Ravioli said, "I see
you have a little something
to share, too, Phoebe."
Everyone giggled.
I wished I still had my star leaf.

I shared the palm tree. Somebody shouted, "What are you bringing next week, a jungle?"
The whole class laughed.

After school I told my mother I wasn't sure I'd ever
bring anything for show-and-tell again.

"Of course you will!" she said. "We'll find something
twice as special next time."

A few days later I found a chicken bone that looked
like it came from a baby dinosaur. I told my parents
I was *thinking* about bringing it for show-and-tell.

They had other ideas.

My parents rented a *Tyrannosaurus rex* skeleton for me to bring to school. They were so excited, they started show-and-tell on the lawn!

Later that morning
Zachary shared a frog
he caught in a market.
He said he found the frog
in the frozen-food section.

Sara shared a leather
saddle. You could smell
horse all over the room.

My parents shared the *Tyrannosaurus rex*. I stood
behind the tailbone. I think they forgot I was there.

For the next show-and-tell I decided to share my Popsicle stick collection. I didn't tell my parents. They had helped enough already.

On the morning of show-and-tell I woke up to a funny sound outside my window.

"Isn't it fantastic?" my mother said. "We got you a lovely herd of cows! We thought you forgot about show-and-tell. We didn't want you to go to school empty-handed."

"Thanks," I said, "but I'm bringing my Popsicle stick collection."

"Take the cows," my mother said, "just in case your Popsicle sticks aren't enough."

Somewhere on the way to class I went left and
the cows must have gone straight. This was great.
I was finally bringing something I wanted to share.

Lily shared a painting
she made of her brother
Arthur. She used chocolate
pudding for paint.

Alyssa shared a book
she read on raising rabbits.
It must have been a good
book because all she had
for lunch was carrots.

When Ms. Ravioli called my name I was excited.
I shared my Popsicle stick collection. Lily asked if
they were from a village in Northern Ooboonie.
"No," I said. "I collected them from Polar Pops."

I told everyone that I loved the way Polar Pops
tasted but I was really more interested in saving
the sticks. I had tried other Popsicles, I told them,
but Polar Pops made the strongest sticks and
they were so smooth I never got a splinter
working with them.

When Ms. Ravioli called my name I was excited.
I shared my Popsicle stick collection. Lily asked if
they were from a village in Northern Ooboonie.
"No," I said. "I collected them from Polar Pops."

I told everyone that I loved the way Polar Pops tasted but I was really more interested in saving the sticks. I had tried other Popsicles, I told them, but Polar Pops made the strongest sticks and they were so smooth I never got a splinter working with them.

I showed my class that by making a tiny notch on the side of a stick, they held together so you could build things.

I brought out the plans I had made to build a
skyscraper.

Ms. Ravioli let the entire class spend the afternoon
working on my skyscraper.

That night, my mother asked how show-and-tell went.
"Great!" I said.
"I knew they would like the cows," said my mother.
"I didn't share the cows," I told her. "I really
appreciated that you and Dad tried to help me. And
the cows were really very nice cows. But I kind of
wanted to bring something I picked for myself."

My mother stopped chewing her peas.

"I shared my Popsicle stick collection," I said.
"Everybody loved it."
My father put down his fork.
"We're going to build a Popsicle stick city," I told
them, "and it was my idea!"

Just then fourteen Polar Pops trucks pulled up in front of our house.

My father asked my mother if she had ordered
the Popsicles.
"No," she told him. "Did you?"

My parents looked at me. I was smiling.
"It seems like you've got some pretty good ideas
of your own," said my father.

My father asked my mother if she had ordered
the Popsicles.
"No," she told him. "Did you?"

My parents looked at me. I was smiling.
"It seems like you've got some pretty good ideas
of your own," said my father.

"Thanks," I said. "I learned from the best!"

"Wait until you see what I'm bringing for
show-and-tell next week!"